THE NIGHT OF THE BEAST

BOOK ONE OF THE REUNION

BY JOSHUA BURNS

ILLUSTRATED BY BILL BRYAN

Order this book online at www.trafford.com
or email orders@trafford.com

Most Trafford titles are also available at major online book retailers.

Printed in the United States of America.

ISBN: 978-1-4269-7372-7

Trafford rev. 06/20/2011

 www.trafford.com

North America & international
toll-free: 1 888 232 4444 (USA & Canada)
phone: 250 383 6864 ✦ fax: 812 355 4082

ACKNOWLEDGEMENTS

I would like to thank my family and friends for all of their love and support throughout the years in which I have been trying to write; even if publishing wasn't anything I expected to be possible.

I would like to thank my fiancée Caitlin for being by my side the whole way and bringing me up when the whole thing was looking down.

I would also like to thank my friend Joey for being the one to actually giving me the final push I needed and to submit one of my many stories that I've wrote throughout the years. He knew I wanted it and helped make it happen, may never have tried if he didn't push it.

Also I would like to thank my grandma for the extra encouragement and showing me all of her own work that she had done throughout her life.

And thank you to my roommate and friend Kris for the support and helping me with the financial part of publishing.

And I can't forget the four guys who showed me what its like to do what you love in life: Joey, Brian, Korey, and Jeff.

A very big thank you to the four who planted the seed that grew to become my imagination in the first place at a very young age: my brother Jason, and friends Dan, Kevin, and Jason. They introduced me to many far away worlds in which I could escape from reality, which inspired me to write in the first place, and on that note I would also like to thank everyone that was or is currently in my gaming group and dealt with all the stories I have put them through no matter how grueling I'm sure they could be at times and continually widening my perspective on how limitless fantasy can be.

For Carter, may the life ahead of you be full of wonders and your dreams come true...mine have

THE NIGHT OF THE BEAST

Book One of the Reunion

The sound of the man's footsteps resonated off the stone street within the walled city, a hollow sound as familiar as his own shadow. The darkness of the night drove away all other sane denizens of the city leaving him alone with whatever was left over and his prey. The autumn moon was his guiding light to seek out the shadow.

The wind blew his long coat around his ankles as he walked. His wide brimmed hat casting a dark shadow over his face, concealing his features except for his bright piercing eyes. With each step various hidden weapons and instruments made a soft clicking sound as they bounced off his legs as he moved.

Rats skittered down the alleys from one heap of midden to another. Quiet sobs of the homeless drifted from somewhere out of the man's field of vision. The cool wind whispered in his ears and twisted his long coat about his legs.

He stopped, listening for the subtle sounds the fiend he was hunting made when feeding. Trying to pick up the scent of blood, and feel the tension of fear. He was close.

He turned down the nearest alley to his right, keeping his right hand hidden within the folds of his coat and his left in one of its large side pockets.

The walls of the buildings on either side of the alley were blocking the moonlight from entering and banishing the darkness they seemed to protect; it wasn't so dark that he couldn't see anything however. He could make out vague shapes of piles of refuse littering the ground, broken glass reflecting the small amount of light the stars could offer, and about halfway down the alley there was a large form lying in a heap on the ground that was not a pile but a single mass of something.

He cautiously made his way down the alley, the lack of light making it seem impossibly longer than it actually was. He had a sick sinking feeling that this was a trap, but after all how effective was a trap when your quarry is prepared for it.

His grip on his hand crossbow tightened as he drew nearer the heap on the ground before him. Whatever it was he could now see it wasn't moving.

He slid his finger to the trigger once he was close enough to see that it was a man, a dead man. Then it was on him. Out of nowhere, without a sound it was behind him. He could feel it's hot breath that came out as shallow rasping sounds and smell the rotting meat that was stuck between its teeth; however the fiend gave off no body heat even though it was practically on top of him.

In one swift motion he crouched, whirled on his heel, pulled a hand crossbow from the folds of his coat with his right hand, and a crucifix from his pocket with his left. The crossbow fired with a dull thwack and pierced the thing's throat, spattering the man's face with dark ichor as he thrust forward his crucifix, searing the dead flesh on its corrupted face.

The silence of the night was broken by shrill howls of agony.

Dry leaves crunched beneath the weight of the wagon as it followed a dirt road down a hill into the small village of rough houses with thatch roofs.

The inhabitants regarded the man in a long coat and wide-brimmed hat riding in the wagon with cold, wary glances, never making eye contact. The fear was almost tangible here. Pulling his long coat tight around him, he decided this was a stop he needed to make.

As he slid off the wagon most of the villagers retreated into their homes or into nearby shops; some merely backed away nervously and continued on with what they were doing before. The people were so consumed by fear they apparently lost any trust for strangers that they once might have had.

The war against humankind's most primordial instinct, fear is waged on two fronts: the mind and the soul. When confronted by something completely unknown one doesn't know how to deal with it, how to overcome it. This is the main reason why villagers won't unite and overcome the things the man hunts on their own. As for the soul, when confronted by something that simply shouldn't be it can wreak havoc within a person.

Fear is what the man thrives on. His eyes scanned the surrounding forest; wondering what could be out there bringing terror on the village, was it watching him even now, in the waning light of the sunset just out of view?

The bright dying rays of the sun's last light enhanced the brilliant colors of the remaining leaves that clung vigorously to the twisted grey-black trees in contrast to the brown, decaying leaves carpeting the forest floor, giving off an eerie beauty.

The leaves remaining on the trees reminded him of people; so desperate to hang on just a little longer, even if they can no longer sustain themselves; always content on prolonging the inevitable before plunging into a world of darkness and decay.

The full moon shone brightly through the skeletal branches of the bare trees, reaching toward the sky like black gnarled claws. Bathing the village in a pale light, its dirt roads deserted and shrouded in silence.

It had been three hours since the man had sat down at an empty table in the village tavern and began listening to the hushed conversations, probing for any word of the abomination and its appearance. Over this time it hadn't been mentioned once, and if he inquired about it the people recoiled in fear, as if the mere mention of it would bring it screaming from the woods in a bloody rage.

It seemed conversation would not be the answer; perhaps it would be best to wait for the beast to strike and go from there.

There was, however the possibility that it wasn't some foul beast, but just a man that lived in the village that was causing all of the village terror. In the case of it being a man it could be more difficult to track but doubtless easier to wrest from him the power granted while wielding fear as a weapon. With that done he would no longer be a threat and the villagers could dispose of him as they see fit.

If it does turn out to be a creature then it would be as simple as a huntsman tracking his prey, a deadly prey. He preferred the beast over the man.

Upon the realization that he wasn't making any progress he made his way to the local inn to retire for the night. Perhaps the next day would bring the answers he sought. He hated doing things this way, he preferred being able to prevent deaths, not use them as tools.

As always, with sleep came fitful dreams of the past; it didn't take long for the man to realize that this was no curse but a blessing in disguise. It no longer brought to him grief but spread a fiery determination through him. It revitalized him more than any amount of sleep ever could.

This night, however was interrupted hours before dawn drove away the darkness of the night. A loud scream pierced through his slumber as an arrow pierces a target, and in a way that's what he was, a target. If he didn't hear it he would have missed his chance.

Bolting out of bed the man gathered his things and ran outside to find the source of the sound. It came again only this time breaking off into a sob, and it was all that was needed for him to make it to the distressed woman.

She was on her knees cradling what was left of whom the man assumed was her husband, rocking back and forth, stroking his hair, Her tears mixing with the dead man's blood ran rivulets down his face. Her heavy green dress flecked red with what must have been the last of his blood judging by the puddle beneath him.

It only took a moment for the man to spot the large abnormal tracks leading back into the forest. This was no man playing off fear; this was indeed some fell beast preying on the innocent.

Without wasting any time with petty sympathies that he knew would make no difference anyway, he strode into the forest, guided by the pale light from the moon and stars above.

The wind carried with it the bittersweet stench of death. As he made his way deeper and deeper into the wood, the potency of the smell increased.

The forest was strangely silent aside from the sounds of the beast ahead, crashing through the underbrush with abandon. Rays of pale moonlight spotted the forest floor where it could penetrate the skeletal canopy above, making visibility low.

The man tried to keep pace, sacrificing a little silence for greater speed. The sound the beast was making would more than cover the man's footsteps. Briars pulled at him and downed trees and exposed roots threatened to trip them but he paid them no heed as he moved.

His heart pounded in exhilaration as he moved. Adrenaline coursed through his body, banishing any weariness that may have been burdening his limbs only moments before when he was taken from his fevered slumber. This was what he lived for.

After what seemed like hours of pursuit the man could finally make out a vague shape ahead of him, scuffing around the underbrush. It was in a clearing in the forest that stretched for about fifteen yards, and was filled with waist high grass and weeds. The world seemed to be cut off by the wall of trees surrounding the two of them, hunter and prey. It was as if nothing else could enter or leave, nothing else mattered, as if everything revolved around this moment. His fevered dreams forgotten and his soul calm, he crouched down for a few moments to see if the creature was aware of his presence.

He could not clearly see the beast for it was obscured by the tall grass, he could tell it was covered in course fur and was on four legs but nothing more of its appearance. By his movements he could tell it was something wild, something primal. It didn't think as a man would, but more like an animal.

Could there be more? He could only hope that it didn't belong to a pack of some sort. The man scanned the clearing for movement in the grass in other areas of the clearing and saw none. He then scanned the tree line around the clearing for anything and found nothing. If it was a member of a pack he was confident that it was alone at the moment, and with much relief it did not notice him yet.

Lowering himself to a crawl he soundlessly made his way closer to get a clear shot, his hand crossbow loaded in one hand, and pulling himself forward with the other. Its foul stench hit him with such force he could almost feel it. He could hear its labored breathing; it was winded from the run. He still could not see it however, being as low as he was the thick tall grass and weeds obscured his view.

Suddenly, he could feel its eyes locked on him. It caught his scent. Time seemed to go from a raging blur of motions to almost a complete halt. Each heart beat sounded like a canon firing and each breathe like a gust of wind.

As the man heard it begin to run off, he swiftly rose up and shot towards its fleeing form. The thing howled in rage and pain as the bolt connected, but after a slight stumble it kept going at great speed.

The man knew he couldn't pursue any longer, he couldn't risk becoming exhausted and battling fatigue along with the beast. He needed to be as strong and ready as he could when hunting the fell creatures of the night.

The best thing to do would be to return to the village and see if the beast would strike again, or perhaps find a blood trail when there was more light; perhaps now that the village wasn't easy prey it wouldn't come back. As the adrenaline started to fade he turned to head back to the village.

The next day there was no difference in the mood of the townsfolk after the attack on the woman's husband. It was as if it was a part of their everyday lives. Whenever he tried explaining he wounded the beast, hoping that the knowledge that the beast could be killed would deal a blow to the reigning fear he was met with snorts and sneers of disproval. Apparently it was all or nothing for these people.

That night the man sat at a small wooden table in his room, staring at the single lantern sitting on the table, its flame dancing to a tune unheard, painting the walls in a myriad of shadows, each an exaggeration of the objects which it was cast from. He was softly humming to the tune of a children's song he used to sing to his son in what seemed like a lifetime ago. If he closed his eyes he could see his son, lying on a bed, blankets pulled snug to his chin.

As he stroked his son's hair he would sing softly as he did every night. It was the man's favorite part of each day, in spite of all the chaos of life; on those nights it always seemed to be a soothing calm. In the way the shadows of a flickering candle played across the boy's face and in the silence of the night.

He could remember his son fighting to stay awake to make it to the end of his favorite song, but he never was able to. He would close his eyes for a few moments and his body would give a slight jerk as he opened them again until he was unable to bear the ever increasing weight of his eye lids. Now his eyes would remain closed forever.

As the years go by certain details have began to deteriorate. Some things came to him blurry, there was hardly anything surrounding his son's bed but a vast void of lost detail. He hoped to be reunited with his wife and son before they began to faded into the void as well. For all the foul things he has hunted that was a greater fear to him than any.

It's been nearly fourteen years since they were taken from him; ripped from his life like a child losing his grip on a kite, watching as it slowly fades away.

He then remembered the day he first met his wife; he was on his way home from an unsuccessful hunting trip in a forest near his home.

In the middle of his hunt it had started to downpour, cutting his visibility considerably low, and made it nearly impossible to pick out any sound of an approaching animal. He remained crouched in a patch of ferns for a few more moments before he decided to give up.

He was walking along a dirt road that was quickly turning into a muddy soup, he was in no hurry considering he was already soaking wet and the rain itself didn't particularly bother him.

Eventually the road rounded a curve and around this curve he spotted a wagon stuck in the road, the rear end was too heavy with the passengers' entire luggage being kept there and buried itself about halfway up the wheels.

There were two men, who looked to be a father and son, trying to free it with wooden planks; off to the side out of the mud were two lovely ladies, who looked to be the mother and daughter of the family, watching in agitation. The bottoms of their dresses were covered in mud which turned into more of a splatter further up the dress, it's dark color greatly contrasting to the bright colors of the clothing beneath.

The daughter was the most beautiful woman the man had ever laid eyes on. Her eyes were bright blue and once caught; your gaze was hopelessly trapped. Her long brown hair flowed like the gentle waves of a river with two tight braids in the front. Her skin was as fair as the moon itself and looked as smooth as silk. He was awe struck.

Hoping to impress her, he strode towards them to help free the wagon. At first the men refused to let him, saying that there was no reason for him to trouble his self with their mishap in this kind of weather. He eventually convinced them to let me help however.

It was no easy task, for even after they removed the luggage and placed it in the ladies' care the wagon was still very heavy and they couldn't get any footing in the mud to lift it high enough to slide the planks beneath the wheels. Somehow they managed to do it and once they could get leverage they were able to free the wagon.

The men of the family then offered him to ride with them and have dinner at their home. With a quick glance toward the younger lady he answered without hesitation and offered his help if they were to get stuck again on the way as well. They informed him that their home wasn't far away and they looked forward to showing their gratitude.

The trip seemed much to short as he was talking to the family and getting to know them better. The young woman was shy at first but didn't take too long to get involved in the conversation with the rest of the family. They asked some questions about him; once answered the man directed the questions toward them. He wanted to know as much as possible before they reached their home for fear of unwittingly offending them over dinner.

It wasn't long before they reached their home. The man couldn't remember much of its appearance other than it was a white farmhouse. He was far more interested in the people that lived within it. They never spent a lot of time there; most of their early time spent together was in the nearby town or in the forest where he taught her how to hunt.

The father of the family welcomed him to his home and showed him where he could wash his hands and face while they prepared dinner.

After doing so he made his way back to the dining room and eagerly awaited the company of the woman who would in later years become his wife.

From this meeting came a close friendship between the man and the family. He and the woman became all but inseparable in a short amount of time. It didn't take long for him to realize his favorite thing about her; her smile. No matter how dark things seemed to look her smile would shine bright and with it her eyes would sparkle, making them more mesmerizing then they already were. A smile that was now forever gone.

A loud crash from downstairs ripped him from his bitter-sweet reverie. His body jerked in surprise, and he was soon on his feet clutching his sword.

A low growl could be heard as well as various thumps that sounded like chairs and tables being overturned, followed by the shattering of glass.

Could it be the beast had tracked him down? He hadn't expected it to have intelligence capable of following him into a building. He reasoned that it was more of a feral beast that acted primarily on instinct.

As he made his way to the door he began to grow frustrated. He had made the mistake he always tried so hard to avoid: he wasn't prepared. There was no time for him to find his other weapons and ready them all; he couldn't risk the safety of the other people staying at the inn. The faster he could resolve this problem the better. He hoped only that if he didn't survive that it would leave and not go on a rampage, tearing apart the other people in the building.

Slowly the wooden door opened with a slight creak as the man opened it and stepped lightly into the empty hallway.

It was lit by flickering lanterns spaced evenly along each wall. There was no sign of anyone else paying any heed to what was going on downstairs. He assumed they were hiding behind closed doors in the false hope that they would stop the creature.

He stepped lightly into the hallway, trying to keep the wooden floor from creaking as he moved slowly toward the stairway that led to the bar downstairs at the end of the hall. He felt as if he were in a dream as he crept past the lanterns posted outside each room. It seemed as though the world had stopped to let the final moments of the hunt to play out undisturbed.

The brief moments in which the moonlight broke through the blanket of cloud would through the shadows askew. He was glad to be in a confined space with no room for the beast to hide in the shifting shadows.

The sounds from below grew silent save for heavy footfalls and an occasional low snarl combined with heavy breathing. It seemed to have relaxed in its search for him. For a brief moment the man considered the possibility of the beast giving up and returning to it's lair within the wood, giving him a better opportunity to kill; he couldn't put the townspeople at that kind of risk however.

As he drew closer to the stairs the abomination's stench assaulted his senses with the force of a tidal wave. It was so strong, so thick that it seemed he could not only smell it but also feel it.

A loud crash broke the silence followed by the sound of splintering wood. The beast had apparently not given up. It sounded as if it had broken into the kitchen to continue its search for him.

He now reached the stairs and peered down into the darkness below; he could make out nothing. No flickering candles or lanterns were fighting off the veil of shadow that all manner of strange things could hide within. He was now in the beast's element and worse, he wasn't at all ready for a confrontation.

He felt no fear however, for if he were to meet his end he would be reunited with his family. He could almost hear them calling to him, see them beckoning.

One slow creaking step at a time he descended into the darkness below each creak of the wooden steps sounded to him like the very earth in its entirety would quake. He knew however, that it was merely his sense deceiving him. Proving unfortunately, his mind was not always an ally.

At the foot of the stairs the barroom loomed before him, a black void sometimes broken by a few stray rays of moonlight, casting everything in a gray color. This light however was never long lasting.

Tables and chairs were splintered and strewn about the room. Claw marks were etched into the walls and the bar, behind which all of the bottles were shattered and all of the barrels broken.

The door to the kitchen was reduced to little more then kindling. From within came the sounds of movement for a few moments before falling into silence.

He slowly crept towards the doorway to the kitchen, mindful of the broken glass and the splinters of wood that once were a part of furniture. It was impossible to avoid it all in the near pitch darkness with only brief illumination at a time, but he knew it would be suicide to get a light source of his own.

His blade remained hidden within its sheath so the light that did occasionally filter through the clouds did not catch the steel of the blade and glint. His gloved hand gripped the sword's black hilt in anticipation, ready to strike when needed.

He was forced to use his other hand for navigating the dark void that was the barroom. One slight bump into anything could be sound enough to alert the beast of his position. He was growing increasingly frustrated however as he would stumble over the broken wood on the floor on occasion.

Once he reached the doorway he put his back to the wall beside the doorway and peered inside. He could see that there was cookware scattered all around the room when the moon provided enough light of see by; though the kitchen window was narrow, preventing the moonlight from illuminating anything more than the center of the room. The rest remained concealed in shadow.

In a heartbeat a large form lurched from within the dark depths of the room and slammed into him as it let out a quick snarl. The force of the blow hurled him backwards into a broken table near the center of the barroom. He could feel something inside him crack as he landed awkwardly.

Winded, he fought his way through the pain and regained his feet, glancing around to find that he was alone; the beast had hidden once more. He ripped his sword from its sheath and made a shaky attempt at a defensive stance. If he played its game there was no way he would survive, he had to draw it out to him if he was to have any chance.

It took several moments for him to somewhat clear his senses once more. The stench remained strong, so he knew it was close. His surroundings ceased spinning, and he could hear it breathing but could not make out where exactly it was because of he was still a little disoriented.

He had to fight to remain standing through the excruciating pain in his ribs. He was sure he had broken one or two bones. He had to find a way to end this quick, if not he wasn't going to last.

Turning towards a sound that seemed to have come from behind the bar to see if he could spot the beast he was met by shards of glass flying towards him. Raising his arm to shield his face the glass was harmlessly turned away by the thick sleeves of his coat.

He lowered his arm to find that there was nothing behind the bar, before the room was cast in total darkness once again.

Spinning this way and that he tried to listen for the sounds of its movement, and heard nothing. The beast managed to avoid all of the wood on the floor and broken glass without so much as the sound of a floor board creaking.

Suddenly, seemingly out of nowhere he felt claws bite deep into the flesh of the back of his left thigh. Dropping to one knee as his leg gave out; he gave a blind off-balanced swing with his sword and nearly fell on his back as he missed.

He wasn't going to give it the satisfaction of showing his frustration with being defenseless against the thing. He decided to stay kneeled fearing he would not be able to keep balanced he tried to stand, and hoping that making himself a smaller target would come to his advantage.

Once again the moonlight turned the room from a black void to a gray wasteland. He tried desperately to spot the beast but to no avail. He was able to see the whole room before it was again consumed in darkness but could not spot his enemy.

Shrouded in darkness once again he could do more than listen and wait. Again he could not hear anything outside of his own labored breathing.

Moments later a crash followed by a piercing scream from above broke the silence. The beast had left him and went upstairs to torment the people hiding in their rooms.

He forced himself to his feet and limped over towards the stairs, stumbling over a broken chair and falling hard to the ground, the impact wrenching his sword from his hand sending it sprawling somewhere within the dark abyss.

There was no time to try to find it, he had to get up the stairs and help the people trapped up there.

Struggling he regained his feet and made it to the foot of the stairs. Using the railing to pull himself he started up, one agonizing step at a time.

The woman's screams continued until they were replaced by a gurgling, rasping sound as he made it about half way up. He could hear what sounded like some wild animal eating its prey; which was broken by the sounds of more screams and footsteps coming toward him.

Before he knew it he was overwhelmed by a crowd of panicking people forcing their way past him down the stairs. He lost his grip in the midst of the pandemonium and fell down the stairs. Someone tripped over him on the way down sending a fiery pain through his already wounded ribs.

Once he hit the floor of the bar, bouncing his head off the hard wood he laid there sprawled out gasping in pain, fighting to get air. His vision was dimming and the sounds of the people grew fainter as they dashed out the door into the night.

He could hear slow heavy footsteps coming toward the stairs from above, accompanied by snarling and heavy breathing. The weight of each step brought dust raining down from above. He turned his head to look up the stairs, waiting for the beast to come finish him off.

The man found himself sitting in a wooden rocking chair in front of a fireplace. His son lay on a thick rug in front of him sleeping, and his wife sat on his lap in his arms. All of his pain was gone.

She gently kissed his cheek and wrapped her arms around his neck embracing him. "Welcome home John." She said with tears in her eyes.

That had been his name...John. He hadn't heard it in so long he had forgotten. He had no need of a name his life was nothing more than a hunt after he lost his family.

He held her tight and kissed her back. He was finally reunited after years of anguish and longing, his chest swelled with the long forgotten feeling of love and happiness.

"I missed you so much", John said as he wept in his wife's arms.

His son woke up from his slumber and upon seeing his father, got up and ran over to him hugging whatever part of John's body he could get to.

"Daddy you're back! Mother said you would be but it has been so long I started to worry you wouldn't be back."

"I'm back son, and I won't be leaving you again." John said, his voice cracking with emotion.

The pain in his ribs and leg began to return slowly. The light of the family slowly gave way to darkness, and his family slowly faded away, startled.

"Daddy please don't leave me again," his son pleaded as he vanished.

He found himself in a bed, his ribs and leg wrapped in bandages and his clothing and weapons placed neatly at the bedside. His son's words stayed with him. His son's expression as he was being taken away once again appeared wherever he looked within the darkness of the room that he was now in.

A single tear ran down his cheek as he realized someone had saved him. Again his family was ripped away from him; his journey was not yet complete.

AN EXCERPT FROM SHADOWS OF THE PAST

Ahead the forest broke away into rolling hills and a few spread out clusters of trees. It had started raining much harder now, and lightning lit the night in flashes offering his surroundings in one quick glimpse at a time followed by the roar of thunder. Was it masking another, more bestial roar in the distance? He thought he heard it but couldn't be sure.

Pressing on through the storm and the pain, trembling he made his way to peak of the nearest hill, slipping on the slick grass on the way.

Amidst the flashes of light he could see a large manor atop another in the distance. Surrounding it was a low stone wall, not meant for protection but only to be decorative.

Large trees were spread out across the property, one of which grew up tight against the house, its branches pushed into the wall. He could make out no more of the layout from his position.

The manor itself seemed to be quite old and abandoned. The windows were dark and the shutters hung loose, and the roof seemed to be in a state of disrepair. He couldn't tell for sure from the distance he was from it however.

If nothing more it would make for shelter for the night; somewhere to ease the pains of his battered body out of the rain. Perhaps there would even be a bed inside waiting for him.

The night sky trembled as he swung open the small wrought iron gate with a screech. Upon closer inspection he could see the manor was in better condition than he had thought. The shutters were secure in their proper place, and nothing was wrong with the roof; another testament as to how weary he was.

If there were any people living in the house confronting them would be something best left for morning. He didn't want to pound on their door at this hour and rouse them only to startle them with his ragged appearance and weapons he carried.

He circled the house on its right side. Between the man and a large barn were several scattered equipment, including a rusted wheelbarrow. Several worn and rusted garden tools were propped up against a post near what could have once been a garden but was now no more than a mass of tall weeds and creepers climbing what was left of the split rail fence that formed the perimeter.

Passing by a large oak tree with a small courtyard formed by a thigh high wrought iron fence containing five grave markers. With a flash of lightning a name was revealed on the one nearest to the man: Jesse Flinn

Continuing on he reached the barn, which was startlingly run down in comparison to the manor. The wood was old and gray with holes in various places where it had rotted through. The door hung off of one hinge and slammed against the side of the barn in the wind.

Once inside the barn, what was left of the roof did little to stop the pouring rain. He was assaulted with a strong musty smell that threatened a headache.

There were six stalls that appeared to once have held an animal, probably a horse, in each. Rusty tools lined the walls, hung on wooden pegs.

Finding a stall that allowed the least rainwater in, he collapsed on the pile of straw, not minding that it was rotten. He kept his weapons near and closed his eyes, feeling the pain in his leg gradually subsiding from being constant to a dull throb. Once his breathing began to come easier it didn't take long for his exhaustion to overcome him.

In his dreams came shards of broken memories. His son's face as he faded away; the same as it did in the vision. Of the battle with the beast. Of the other creatures he had hunted and slain in the past. Of his wife's smile; a smile that could melt the blackest darkness.

These nightmares that so often haunted his sleep were what invigorated him for the tasks ahead. They were a nightly reminder of why he hunted the creatures of darkness. They filled him with a purpose that nothing else could match.

JOSH BURNS IS A YOUNG AUTHOR FROM THE SMALL TOWN OF CARO MICHIGAN. HE ENJOYS MUSIC, PAINTBALL GAMING, AND WRITING.